Hans Christian Andersen

The Little Mermaid

and other fairy tales

Miles
KeLLy

First published in 2015 by Miles Kelly Publishing Ltd
Harding's Barn, Bardfield End Green, Thaxted, Essex, CM6 3PX, UK

2 4 6 8 10 9 7 5 3 1

Publishing Director Belinda Gallagher
Creative Director Jo Cowan
Editorial Director Rosie Neave
Editor Amy Johnson
Designers Rob Hale, Joe Jones
Production Manager Elizabeth Collins
Reprographics Stephan Davis, Jennifer Cozens, Thom Allaway

ISBN 978-1-78209-751-8

Printed in China

British Library Cataloguing-in-Publication Data
A catalogue record for this book is available from the British Library

ACKNOWLEDGEMENTS
The publishers would like to thank the following artists who have contributed to this book:

Front cover and all border illustrations: Louise Ellis (The Bright Agency)

Inside illustrations:
The Little Mermaid Claudia Venturini (Plum Pudding Illustration Agency)
The Windmill Martina Peluso (Advocate-art)
The Story of the Year Lucia Masciullo (Pickled Ink)
The Flea and the Professor Mónica Carretero (Plum Pudding Illustration Agency)

Made with paper from a sustainable forest

www.mileskelly.net
info@mileskelly.net

Contents

The Little Mermaid

Far out in the ocean, where the water is as blue as cornflowers, it is very, very deep. There live the most lovely sea creatures and plants. In the deepest spot of all was a castle where the Sea King lived with his six daughters. The sea princesses were all beautiful mermaids, but the youngest was loveliest of all.

Every day, the sea princesses played happily in the castle or outside. Each mermaid had a little garden to tend as she pleased. The youngest mermaid grew flowers around the statue of a handsome boy that had fallen from a shipwreck. She loved to hear about the world above – for the sea princesses were not allowed to the surface to see it for themselves until they were fifteen. The little mermaid made her grandmother tell her everything she knew about ships, towns, forests, people and animals.

Finally, the youngest princess's fifteenth

birthday came. How excited she was to rise to the surface, light as a bubble! She raised her head above the waves and gasped as she saw a grand ship floating in the glorious sunset. The little mermaid swam close and peered in through the cabin windows. She saw lots of people inside, eating and drinking and dancing. Among them was a handsome young prince – it was his birthday party. As darkness drew in, the people came out on deck to admire magnificent fireworks bursting in the sky.

The mermaid watched, fascinated, until it grew late. But then heavy clouds gathered, thunder roared and lightning flashed, and the waves towered into dark mountains.

A terrible storm tossed and tipped the ship, until suddenly it plunged over on its side. Everyone was washed into the water!

To the little mermaid's horror, she saw the handsome prince sinking. His beautiful eyes were closed and she knew he was about to die. She dived down and used all her strength to lift him and hold his head above the water.

When the sun rose, the little mermaid swam to a sandy bay and laid the prince in the shallows. She stroked his wet hair and kissed his forehead – he seemed just like the statue in her garden. Then some girls came out of a nearby building, so the little mermaid hid between some rocks. She watched as one of them spotted the prince and ran to him.

The mermaid saw him open his eyes and smile. Then the girl helped him up and led him away.

The little mermaid swam sorrowfully back to her father's castle. From then on, her heart was filled with longing for the prince and the world above. 'I will see if the sea witch can help me,' she thought.

The way to the sea witch's home was very dangerous. It lay through whirlpools, boiling mud and poisonous plants. When the brave little mermaid arrived, the witch said: "I know what you want. I will change your fish's tail into legs, so you can walk on land and find your prince. But every step will be as painful as treading on knives – and you will never be able to return to the sea and your family again. If the prince falls in love with you and marries you, you will become properly human, with a soul that will live in heaven after you die. But if he marries another girl, at sunrise on the next day your heart will break and you will become foam on the waves."

"I will do it," said the little mermaid, determinedly.

"But I must be paid," said the witch. "You have the sweetest voice in the ocean. Give it to me."

"So be it," the little mermaid whispered.

The sea witch placed her cauldron on the fire, dropped in many evil ingredients and prepared a magic potion in a bottle. She held up another one and conjured the mermaid's voice out into it, so she could enjoy it forever. Then the little mermaid silently took the magic potion and rose up, up, up, through the dark blue waters.

The moon shone brightly over the sandy bay, as the little mermaid floated in the shallows and drank the magic potion. It hurt as badly as if she were swallowing fire, and she fainted.

When the sun rose, the mermaid came to. She was lying on the sand and before her stood the handsome young prince, smiling. She looked down shyly, and realized that her fish's tail was gone. Instead, she had a pretty pair of legs and feet and she was wearing clothes. The prince asked who she was and where she came from, but the mermaid just looked at him sorrowfully, for she could not speak. He helped her to stand and walk, and every step she took was painful, but she didn't mind.

The prince took her back to the palace and looked after her, for she was the most beautiful girl he had ever seen. He was totally charmed by her and told her that she would stay with him always. The days passed and the little mermaid was overjoyed to be spending time with the prince – she only wished she could tell him.

But one morning, the little mermaid woke to hear church bells. "Today is my wedding day," the prince explained. "My father has ordered that I get married, to a girl who saved my life when I lay half-drowned on the beach."

The little mermaid felt as though her heart were already broken.

The wedding was held on a magnificent ship out at sea. The little mermaid was a bridesmaid and wore a gold silk dress. But she didn't hear the music playing or see the colourful flags. Her mind was filled with everything she had given up, and of dying and becoming foam on the waves.

Late that night, the prince and his bride went to their cabin. The little mermaid turned to where the sun would rise and waited for the morning, when she was going to die.

As the first ray of dawn lit the sky, the little mermaid threw herself into the sea – but her body did not dissolve into foam. The sun rose and all around her floated beautiful transparent beings. The little mermaid suddenly realized that her body was like theirs, and she soared up into the sky.

"We are spirits," one of the beings

explained. "We fly around the world doing good deeds. When we have done enough, we are granted a soul and go to live in heaven. You, little mermaid, have been chosen to join us, as you gave up everything you held dear for love."

The little mermaid's heart was filled with joy. She left the prince and his bride behind her, and flew away with the spirits to win her soul and be happy in heaven for ever.

The Windmill

A long time ago, in a land far away, there stood on a hill a stately windmill. It had been there as long as anyone could remember and looked rather like it was growing out of the countryside. People might have thought that it just stood there with its sails creaking round and round, but actually, the windmill spent its days thinking deeply.

"I am very lucky," she said to herself one morning, "that people like looking at me. To start with, I always have bright eyes. Either the sun's rays or the moonbeams shine at my windows, or the miller lights them up with candles and lanterns. I have four graceful wings – even the birds only have two. And I have a good set of millstones and wheels in my chest. There is a gallery that runs like a patterned belt around my stomach, and in my heart, the miller and his wife live. Their little children are like thoughts that run around my head. Indeed, the family keep me alive – I remember that lately I had to let the miller and his boys examine my millstones, for something was wrong. They knew just how to make me better. Then the youngest climbed up into my hat and shouted out, and it tickled me!

"Out in the world, I can't see anything like me. I can see houses but they just look wingless and strange.

"I have been here for many years and seen many things. And I know that the days pass, and the days come, and the time will arrive when I will tumble down. But I will be built up again. I will look different, but as long as I have the miller and his wife living at my heart, and the children running around me like thoughts, I will be the same inside. And everyone will say: 'There's the mill on the hill – what a sight to see.'"

And so the days passed, and the days came, and one afternoon the mill caught fire. The flames shot up and whipped in and out. They licked beams and ate up planks. The mill crumbled to ash and thick smoke rose from the embers until the wind carried it all away.

Very luckily, the miller's family had not been at home at the time. They were filled with sadness to lose the old mill, but they soon built a beautiful new mill. And the miller and his wife lived at its heart and their little children ran around it like thoughts. Its windows were always lit, and its sails creaked steadily round and round while it stood, thinking deeply. And everyone said: "There's the mill on the hill – what a sight to see."

The Story of the Year

It was near the end of January. Thick snow was falling, whirling through the streets. All day it fell. Then the skies cleared, the people came out of their houses and the soft snow crunched under their feet.

Sparrows flew down and hopped along the ground, looking for food. They were terribly cold. "Tweet, tweet," said one. "People call this a new year, but I think it is just as bad as the last one!"

"Yes," remarked another sparrow. "In fact, it's colder than ever. I think people have made a mistake – this can't be a new year at all."

"I agree," said a third sparrow, the smallest. "I know the people have something called a calendar. They invented it and they organize everything by it. But I think they've got it wrong. When spring comes, the new year begins – that's what nature says, and that's what I say too!"

"When will spring come?" said another.

"I'm not sure," replied the little sparrow. "The country birds know more about these things than us town birds. Let's go to the fields and ask them." And away they flew.

In the countryside it was even more wintry. The sparrows hopped about in a frozen field and cried, "Tweet! When will spring come? It is taking a very long time."

"Very long indeed," came a voice. It was an old man with a pale face and long white hair, dressed in grey, sitting on a mound of snow.

"Who is that?" wondered the sparrows.

"It is Winter, the ruler of last year," said an old raven, sitting on a fence. "He is not dead yet, even though the calendar says he is."

"There! I told you so!" said the smallest of the sparrows.

One week passed, and then another, and another. Then one morning, two storks came flying from the south. On the back of each sat a lovely little child – a boy and a girl.

The storks landed in the field and the two children slipped off their backs and kissed the earth.

Wherever they placed their feet, tiny

white flowers sprang up from beneath the snow. Hand in hand they approached the old ice-man, Winter, and hugged him. As they did so, the sun shone warmly. Winter vanished, leaving the two children – the Prince and Princess of Spring.

"Now this is really the new year," cried all the sparrows. "Hooray!"

Wherever the two children wandered, buds sprouted on bushes and trees. The grass grew higher and the cornfields sprang up green.

The little girl scattered seeds from her pockets and flowers sprang into life. The boy clapped his hands and flocks of birds came flying, singing, "Spring has come!" The children laughed as gentle rain fell upon them from the sky and they ran off, playing.

Days and weeks went by and the weather grew warmer. By the wall of a farmhouse sat a young man and a young woman – they were the two children, who had grown up, becoming the Lord and Lady of Summer.

The cornfields glittered golden yellow. The branches of trees dipped with heavy fruit, and the bees buzzed around the flowers.

Sometimes, thunder and lightning flashed and steamy showers fell, clearing the heat from the air for a while.

"Do you remember," the woman said one day, "how we travelled to this land as children? We played then, and were full of energy. Everything is good now, but – I don't know why – I long for peace and rest."

Just then storks appeared overhead, flying away to the south. The man and woman lifted up their arms to them and vanished.

"Tweet – where have they gone?" chirped

the sparrows, as the leaves on the trees changed from green to colours of red, brown and gold. And out of the forest strode the Lord of Autumn. He smiled and lifted his arm.

Fresh winds swept through the trees and the leaves fell in showers. Chestnuts dropped in their prickly shells to the ground. Mists dampened the earth.

Weeks passed and the evenings grew longer and darker. The air became colder and more crisp. There came a time when snowflakes fell from the sky and turned the Lord of Autumn's bronze hair to white. He had become Winter, ruler of the year. With his pale face and grey clothes, he went to rest on a snowy mound, clenching his fists.

Then came the sparrows again out of the town, and asked, "Who is that?"

And the raven on the fence said to them: "It is Winter, the ruler of last year. He is not dead yet, even though the calendar says he is."

"There! I told you so!" said the smallest sparrow. "When will spring come?"

One week passed, and then another. Then one morning, two storks came flying from the south…

And that is the story of the year. Although it is not according to the calendar, so it may all be wrong.

The Flea and the Professor

There was once a lad who taught himself how to speak without moving his lips. He could make it seem as if his voice came out of all sorts of objects, and it didn't look as though he was talking at all.

When he was a young man, he earned a living by travelling around performing a ventriloquism show – that is to say, he had a couple of puppets whom he used to make talk while his own mouth never moved. People were astounded, especially when he began doing magic tricks too. Young ladies were enchanted by him – one of them even ran away with him to a foreign country. There, the young man called himself 'the professor', to make himself sound very clever and impressive.

But the professor longed for something more than becoming a famous ventriloquist. His secret dream was to own a hot air balloon and fly around the world with his wife. However, even though he worked hard, he never managed to save enough money.

The professor's wife was just as excited about the hot air balloon dream as he was. She helped him as much as she could. First of all, she would sit at the doors of theatres to sell tickets for his shows – which in the wintertime was very chilly! She was also his beautiful assistant in his act. The professor would put her into a large box and shut the lid – then she would creep into a hidden compartment. When the professor opened the box, the audience thought she had turned invisible! It was his clever trick.

But one evening, when the professor opened the box, his wife had turned invisible to him too. She was not in the box, or the hidden compartment, and she was not in the theatre. She was nowhere to be seen or heard – and that was *her* clever trick.

She had run off and never came back. She was tired of having to smile on stage when she felt fed up, and never having enough money to buy a hot air balloon.

After she left, the professor became very sad. The sparkle went out of his eyes and his shoulders drooped. He didn't feel like talking to anyone any more, let alone being cheery and entertaining on stage and performing magic and ventriloquism. His shows stopped being fun, so people stopped coming to see him. He stopped making any money, so he sold all his possessions to buy food. Eventually his clothes became ragged and he grew dreadfully thin.

All the professor had left was a large flea whom he had taught to do tricks. It could juggle with five apple pips at once. It could walk across a highwire strung between two matchboxes. Finally, it could shoot a tiny gun while blindfolded – and always hit its target.

The professor was very proud of the flea and the flea was very proud of himself. He had performed in front of all sorts of important, famous people – royalty too – and he knew that the professor depended upon him to scrape a few coins together. The flea and the professor were extremely fond of each other. They made a secret pact that neither of them would marry and they would never be parted from each other.

With the flea by his side, the professor travelled all over the world, leaving towns and cities behind him and venturing into deathly deserts, up icy mountains and through far-flung jungles.

One day they came to a place where there lived a tribe of people who liked to eat strangers! The professor wasn't very worried because he knew he could charm them with the flea. So the flea did his act and the audience were delighted.

The people showered the professor with gifts of food and toe rings and spears. However, the princess who ruled the tribe decided she would keep the flea as her pet. She didn't ask the professor, she just told him. "Give me the flea or I will eat you!" she said.

The professor couldn't see that he had a choice, so he had to put up with the flea becoming the princess's pet. She took a hair from her head and fastened one end around the flea's leg and the other end around her earring. The flea could perch on her shoulder or her head, but he was her prisoner. How miserable he was!

The tribe made it clear that the professor was free to continue on his travels. But he would not leave and abandon the flea, so he told them he would like to stay for a while. The tribespeople gave him a large hut to live in, with walls made of sugar cane. They brought him lizards and nuts and birds' eggs to eat. Every day, the professor swung in his hammock and racked his brains as to how he could rescue the flea. At last he had an idea…

He went to the princess and told her that he would teach her to fire a cannon. "What's a cannon?" said the princess. And the professor described a hot air balloon.

"You sit in the basket and set it off with a bang!" he fibbed.

"Ooh, yes – I want to set it off with a bang," she cried, her eyes gleaming.

"Well, give me the materials to make a cannon and I will teach you how," the professor said. He asked for fine silk cloth, a needle and thread, ropes and a large woven basket. The princess made sure he had everything he needed.

The professor worked hard for weeks and finally it was ready. He did not call the princess to see the balloon until it was filled with hot air and ready to go up. "I must take the cannon up to cool it off before we can fire it," the professor told her. "But I'm afraid I cannot steer it alone – I need a trained companion to help. There is no one who can do that except the flea."

The princess grumbled and moaned, but in the end she reluctantly untied the flea from her earring and gave him to the professor.

Quickly, he cut the ropes attaching the balloon to the

ground – and away he soared with the flea.

The princess and her family and all of her subjects sat and waited. As far as I know, they are waiting there still. Meanwhile, the professor and the flea became rich and famous hot air balloonists.